Special thanks to
Emily Sharratt

Reading Consultant: Prue Goodwin, lecturer in literacy and children's books.

ORCHARD BOOKS

First published in 2020 by The Watts Publishing Group

5 7 9 10 8 6 4

A CIP catalogue record for this book is available from the British Library.

ISBN 978 1 40835 743 9

Printed and bound in China

The paper and board used in this book are made from wood from responsible sources.

Orchard Books
An imprint of Hachette Children's Group
Part of The Watts Publishing Group Limited
Carmelite House, 50 Victoria Embankment, London EC4Y 0DZ

An Hachette UK Company
www.hachette.co.uk
www.hachettechildrens.co.uk

SCHOOL
TRIP

ORCHARD

MEET ASH AND PIKACHU!

ASH
A Pokémon dreamer who wants to have it all – including becoming a Pokémon Master!

PIKACHU
Ash's first partner Pokémon and long-time companion!

LOOK OUT FOR THESE POKÉMON

GYARADOS

POPPLIO

ALOLAN VULPIX

PSYDUCK

JIGGLYPUFF

CONTENTS

PART ONE: ALOLA, KANTO

PART TWO: OLD FRIENDS AND RIVALS

PART THREE: THE CERULEAN GYM

PART ONE
Alola, Kanto

CHAPTER ONE

A Special Field Trip

Ash's class at the Pokémon School were listening to the Principal, Samson Oak, make an announcement.

"It is the twentieth anniversary of the Pokémon School.

As part of the festivities, I am pleased to tell you that we are going on a special field trip."

The class cheered.

"Does that mean we're going somewhere really amazing?" Ash asked in excitement.

"It certainly does," said their class teacher Professor Kukui. "We're going to Kanto!"

The class cheered again, but Ash's mouth dropped open.

"Kanto?" he said in disbelief. What was so exciting about that?

"Hey, Ash," said Kiawe, one of his new friends in Alola, "isn't that where you're from?"

"Yeah," Ash replied gloomily.

"While we're over there you're going to be having some very special experiences — ones you can't have in Alola," Professor Kukui said. "I think even you will find them challenging, Ash."

Ash looked up hopefully. He did love a challenge.

By the time they arrived in Kanto, Ash couldn't wait to show his friends around. They were all talking about the Pokémon they hoped to see.

Suddenly, Ash stopped as he saw two very familiar faces. "Brock! Misty!" he cried.

Ash ran towards his old friends.

CHAPTER TWO
Brock and Misty

"Hey, Ash!"

Ash's Alolan friends looked on, puzzled, as he hugged Brock and Misty.

"These are friends of mine from Kanto," Ash explained.

"We've had many adventures together," Ash said.

Ash introduced Brock and Misty to his friends from Alola: Kiawe, Sophocles, Lillie, Lana and Mallow, as well as Samson Oak and Professor Kukui.

"What are you doing here?" Ash asked Brock and Misty.

"Professor Oak asked us to come and collect you," Brock answered.

Misty nodded. "We've got some exciting surprises for you and your friends," she added.

"That's right," said Mr Oak. "We should go and see my cousin now."

Little did Ash and his friends know but they were being watched by Jessie, James, Meowth and Wobbuffet – otherwise known as Team Rocket!

"It sounds as though they're heading to Professor Samuel Oak's Laboratory," said Jessie.

"The perfect place to steal a load of top Pokémon," James agreed.

"Then, what are we waiting for?" said Meowth. "Let's go!"

At Professor Oak's laboratory, Brock and Misty were showing Ash's friends around.

"This is ideal for gathering lots of Pokémon data," said Ash's Rotom Dex excitedly.

"Wow!" said Kiawe. "A Rapidash. They're . . ."

"The Fire Horse Pokémon," finished Rotom Dex helpfully.

"Rapidash loves to gallop. When it sees something going fast, it can't resist the urge to race," explained Rotom Dex.

"Is that right?" said Kiawe, drawing out his Poké Ball. "OK, then. Charizard, let's go!"

Kiawe's Charizard burst out with a mighty roar.

"Want to race?" Kiawe called.

CHAPTER THREE

Professor Oak's Laboratory

Rapidash nodded its head and
Kiawe leaped onto Charizard's
back.

As they raced along beside
the Rapidash, it whinnied at
Kiawe.

"Really?" Kiawe said. "You
want me to hop on? OK, then!"

With that, Kiawe flung himself onto the Fire Horse Pokémon's back.

"This is amazing!" he cried, as he was carried off into the distance.

The others were looking at all the different Pokémon.

"A real Vileplume!" exclaimed Mallow.

"Be careful, Mallow," Misty shouted in alarm. "Vileplume's pollen is poisonous!"

"Argh!" cried Mallow, running away.

After a while, Misty and
Brock gathered them all back
together.

"We're going to demonstrate
the differences between some
Pokémon from Alola and
Kanto," said Brock.

From two Poké Balls burst
Exeggutor – one from Alola
and one from Kanto.

"Wow, Kanto Exeggutor are
so short!" said Sophocles.

"It's because they don't get as
much sun here," said Lillie.

"Check these out," said Misty.

She released a Marowak from Kanto and one from Alola.

As soon as the two Pokémon appeared, they turned to each other and began fighting.

"No fighting!" cried Brock.

"Well, they're certainly as short-tempered as each other," said Lana.

The others tried to wrestle the two Pokémon apart.

When the humans had no luck, the other Pokémon tried to help but the two Marowak were determined to fight.

Eventually, Pikachu lost its temper.

With a loud, "Pika-chu!" it used a powerful Thunderbolt move. It was so strong that it knocked everyone to the ground!

PART TWO
Old Friends and Rivals

CHAPTER FOUR

Team Rocket Attack

A little while later Lana asked,
"Where's Popplio?"

Everyone looked but there
was no sign of Popplio.

"Don't worry, Lana," said
Misty. "There's a lake up ahead,
I bet that's where Popplio is."

"Good idea," said Lana.

As they approached the lake, a huge Gyarados burst out of the water, roaring. The friends jumped back, screaming.

Lana laughed. "I'm still going to look," she said, taking off her clothes to reveal a swimming costume underneath. She dived into the water.

"I like this girl," declared Misty, jumping in after her.

Beneath the water were all sorts of beautiful and exciting Pokémon.

Lana swam happily from one to the next, before spotting Popplio, who was playing with some Horsea.

Later that day, the friends all met back at the entrance to Professor Oak's Laboratory.

"Well, I'm glad we're all back together," said Misty, smiling at Popplio.

Suddenly a crashing noise
made them all look up. A
giant robotic Meowth was
thundering towards them.

"What on earth . . .?" said
Ash.

A net dropped down from the
robot Meowth, capturing all
the Pokémon!

It dragged the Pokémon up to its open hatch.

"You mean who on earth," called James from inside the machine.

"And the answer is: who else?" added Jessie, from beside him.

"Team Rocket!" Jessie and James cried together.

CHAPTER FIVE

Battle With Robo-Meowth

"Ugh, you again!" Misty said in disgust.

"You know them too?" asked Sophocles.

"Oh, yes," agreed Brock. "They're old rivals of ours. Give our Pokémon back!"

"They're our Pokémon now,"
called Jessie.

"There's no point asking,"
Ash said, pulling out a Poké Ball.
"Lycanroc, I choose you!"

Ash's Lyranroc burst out,
snarling.

"Use Rock Throw!" Ash cried. Lycanroc fired rubble towards the robot Meowth but the robot just put up its metallic arms and knocked it back.

"Crobat!" yelled Brock.

"Staryu!" shouted Misty, and their Pokémon joined the fight.

"Lycanroc, use Accelerock!" said Ash. His Pokémon threw itself at the robot, knocking it backwards.

Robo-Meowth's massive paw launched towards Lycanroc.

Crobat used its Supersonic move, blocking the attack.

"Use Bubble Beam!"
Misty called to Staryu. Her Pokémon's bubbles hit the robot until it short-circuited and then exploded!

It released the captured
Pokémon.

"Pikachu!" Ash cried happily,
hugging his Pokémon.

Team Rocket stumbled out
of their Robo–Meowth.
Then Bewear appeared and
scooped them up in its arms.

The Strong Arm Pokémon
ran away still holding
Team Rocket.

"Wh-what just happened?"
Brock stammered. Before
anyone could answer him, the
wreckage of the robot began to
rustle.

Ash and his friends drew
backwards. What new danger
were they about to face?

CHAPTER SIX

Jigglypuff's Song

The creature that emerged was small, pink and round, with a smile on its face.

"Is that a real Jigglypuff?" Sophocles asked in delight.

"It's so sweet!" exclaimed Lillie.

"What's that in its hands?" asked Mallow curiously.

"Oh no," said Ash, as he, Brock and Misty all stepped backwards. "Guys, you need to cover your ea—"

But it was too late. As Ash was speaking, Jigglypuff held the microphone to its mouth and began to sing.

"Ji-ggly-puff, Jigglyyyyypuff. Ji-ggly-puff, Jigglyyyy . . ." It sang softly. A moment later, Ash and his friends were fast asleep on the ground.

"Ha ha ha," Ash laughed. He pointed at Kiawe's face, which now had a beard and big eyebrows drawn on.

"I don't know what you're laughing at," Kiawe said.

"I'm not sure whiskers really suit you," Kiawe added.

Ash and his friends looked around at each other. Jigglypuff had drawn on all of their faces while they were asleep!

"Jiggypuff!" they all cried, and then started giggling.

The next day Ash and his friends were in for a big surprise – they were going to the Cerulean Gym!

There they could practise Pokémon battles. Misty was Gym Leader there.

"Welcome to the Cerulean Gym, everybody!" she said. "Trainers in the Kanto region travel to Gyms, battling the Gym Leaders." Misty said.

"When you win, you earn a Badge. There are eight Badges to be won in total." Misty explained.

"And when you've won them all," Ash added, "you can compete in the Pokémon League!"

PART THREE
The Cerulean Gym

CHAPTER SEVEN

Misty vs Mallow and Lana

"What's the Pokémon League?" asked Mallow.

"It's a big tournament where all the best Pokémon Trainers battle each other," Ash replied.

"We don't have anything like that in Alola," Lana said.

"For now," Professor Kukui said. "Let's get started with some practice battles."

"Yeah!" everyone cheered.

"OK, Lana and Mallow, do you want to try your chances against Misty?"

"Yes please!" they said.

"OK, let's see what you can do!" Misty cried, as they all leaped into the battle ring.

"All right, Steenee, use Magical Leaf!" called Mallow.

Misty's Psyduck backed away from Steenee's shooting leaves.

"Popplio, use Bubble Beam!" shouted Lana. Popplio's bubbles knocked Psyduck right onto its back.

"Psyduck, use Water Gun," was Misty's response.

But Popplio was too quick.

It blew a giant balloon that sucked up all of Psyduck's water.

"Go, Popplio!" Lana cheered.

"That's a clever trick, Lana," Misty said, sounding impressed, "but what are you going to do with it now?"

"Balloon, launch!" Lana cried.

Popplio used its tail to bat a balloon over to Psyduck. The balloon sucked it inside.

"Use Magical Leaf again, Steenee!" called Mallow, seeing an opportunity.

Steenee's leaves pelted the giant balloon, making it pop. Psyduck was dropped down to the ground, landing on its head.

CHAPTER EIGHT

Brock vs Sophocles and Lillie

"Oops, sorry!" said Mallow anxiously.

"Don't worry," said Misty. "Psyduck will be fine. And it's at its best in a challenge."

Sure enough, Psyduck was back on its feet.

Psyduck's eyes glowed with a new determination.

"Psy . . . Psy . . ." it began. "Psyduck!" And with that it shook its head, using the Confusion move.

Steenee and Popplio were lifted up into the air, unable to make another move.

After a few moments, Misty said gently, "I think you can let them down again now, Psyduck."

"Yes, that's them out of action," Professor Kukui agreed.

Looking a bit embarrassed, Psyduck carefully lowered the other two Pokémon back to the ground.

"Well done, you two," Misty said. "You showed great battle instincts!"

"Thanks," replied Mallow.

"I feel more confident already," said Lana.

"Come on," said Brock to Sophocles and Lillie, "it's our turn now!"

"Yeah, let's go!" said Sophocles nervously.

"Togedemaru, use Zing Zap!" Sophocles cried.

His Togedemaru built up a huge electric charge, then went spinning towards Brock's Geodude.

"Yeah!" shouted Sophocles and Lillie.

The two Pokémon collided
with a bang. But when they
looked again, Geodude was
fine!

"Geodude," it remarked
calmly.

CHAPTER NINE

The Pokémon League

"What?" said Sophocles in shock. "Zing Zap didn't do a thing! Electric moves should have some effect, Geodude is a Rock- and Electric- type."

"Ah, you're thinking of Alolan Geodudes," Brock

said. "Geodude from Kanto are Rock- and Ground-type Pokémon – Electric moves have no effect on them."

"Oh, no," said Sophocles. "What a miscalculation!"

"Don't worry, Sophocles," said Lillie. "Leave everything to us! Snowy," Lillie called to a Vulpix, "use Powder Snow!"

Snowy drew a deep breath and blew a blizzard towards Geodude.

"Gyro Ball, Geodude!" cried Brock.

Geodude spun in a crackling ball of energy, repelling the snow.

"Wow, I've never seen Gyro Ball used as a defence move!" said Sophocles, his eyes wide.

"Brock wins!" declared Professor Kukui. "Do you see how much there is to learn from Pokémon battles?" he asked his Alolan students.

They all nodded, their eyes shining with excitement.

"That's why I'm determined to make the Pokémon League part of Alola's traditions," said Professor Kukui, looking to see how they'd react.

"That's a brilliant idea!" said Ash, and the others nodded and cheered.

"It's been great getting our gang back together," Brock said to Ash and Misty.

"You're right," Ash agreed. "And next it's your turn to come and visit me in Alola."

"We definitely will, Ash," Misty said.

"You can count on it," Brock added. "Sounds as though you might need our help setting up an Alolan Pokémon League!"

The End

DON'T MISS THESE OTHER OFFICIAL POKÉMON BOOKS